For Ernesto — D.C.
For Magali — S.M.

This edition published by Kids Can Press in 2017

Originally published in French under the title *Petit Pois*.
Text © 2016 Davide Cali
Illustrations © 2016 Sébastien Mourrain

Published with the permission of Comme des géants inc.,
6504, av. Christophe-Colomb, Montreal (Quebec) H2S 2G8

Translation rights arranged through VeroK Agency, Spain
English translation © 2017 Kids Can Press

Kids Can Press gratefully acknowledges the financial support of the Government of Ontario,
through the Ontario Media Development Corporation; the Ontario Arts Council; the Canada Council
for the Arts; and the Government of Canada, through the CBF, for our publishing activity.

Published in Canada and the U.S. by Kids Can Press Ltd.
25 Dockside Drive, Toronto, ON M5A 0B5

Kids Can Press is a Corus Entertainment Inc. company

www.kidscanpress.com

The artwork in this book was rendered in pencil crayon and then colored digitally.
The text is set in Baskerville.

Original edition edited by Nadine Robert and Mathieu Lavoie
English edition edited by Yvette Ghione
Designed by Mathieu Lavoie

Printed and bound in Shenzhen, China, in 3/2017 by C&C Offset

CM 17 0 9 8 7 6 5 4 3 2 1

Library and Archives Canada Cataloguing in Publication

Calì, Davide, 1972–
[Petit pois. English]
The tiny tale of Little Pea / written by Davide Cali ; illustrated by Sébastien Mourrain.

Translation of: Petit pois.
ISBN 978-1-77138-843-6 (hardback)

I. Mourrain, Sébastien, 1976–, illustrator II. Title. III. Title: Petit pois. English.

PZ7.C1283Tin 2017   j843'.92   C2016-906427-1

The Tiny Tale

of Little
Pea

Davide Cali

Sébastien Mourrain

Kids Can Press

When he was born, Little Pea was tiny.
Teeny-tiny.

His clothes?
His mother sewed them by hand.

His shoes?
He wore the dolls' hand-me-downs.

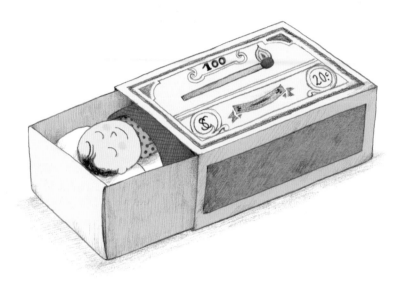

His bed?

It depended.

He taught himself to swim at a very young age.

As Little Pea grew older, he enjoyed wrestling,

climbing,

tightrope walking

and driving his wind-up car.

In the summer, he explored the back garden,

where he took leisurely strolls

and swam in the frog pond.

Sometimes he would float on a lily pad, where he would
daydream and marvel at the size of the universe.

He also liked reading,

climbing tomato plants

and riding
horseback …
well, not quite!

It wasn't until Little Pea started school
that he realized he was too small.

Too small for his chair …

too small to play the flute …

too small for gym class …

even too small for his plate!

At recess, Little Pea kept to himself.

He spent his time drawing.

Poor Little Pea. What will become of him?
his teacher wondered.

And then Little Pea grew up.
(But not much bigger.)

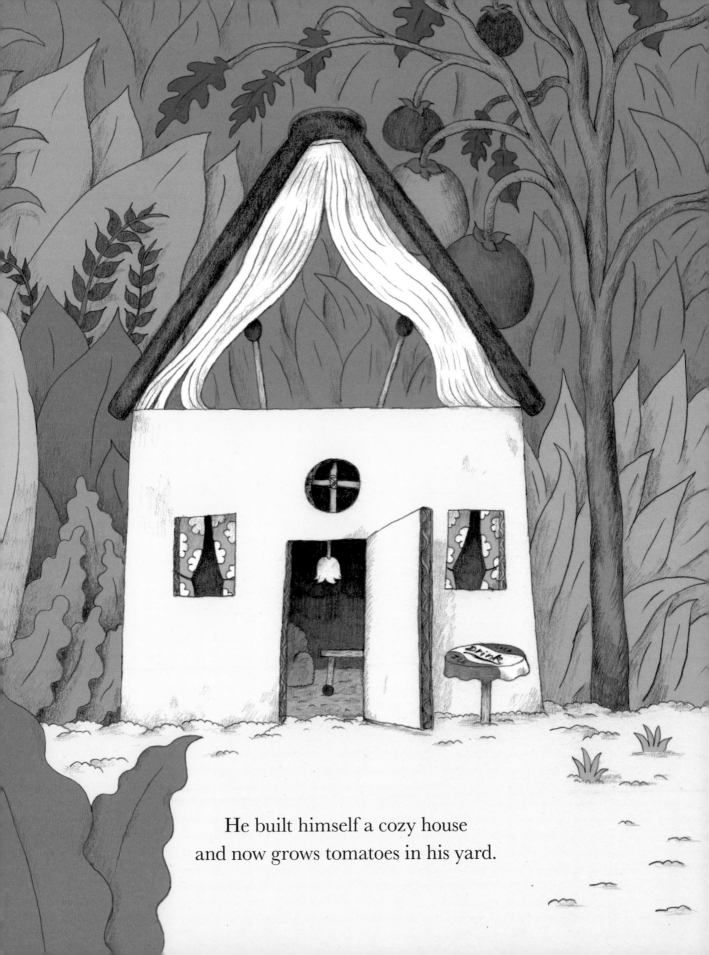

He built himself a cozy house
and now grows tomatoes in his yard.

He rides his car to work every day.

Everything in his studio
has been custom-made just for him.

And do you know what Little Pea's job is?
You'll never guess!

He draws stamps!

One can never be too small
to be a GREAT artist!